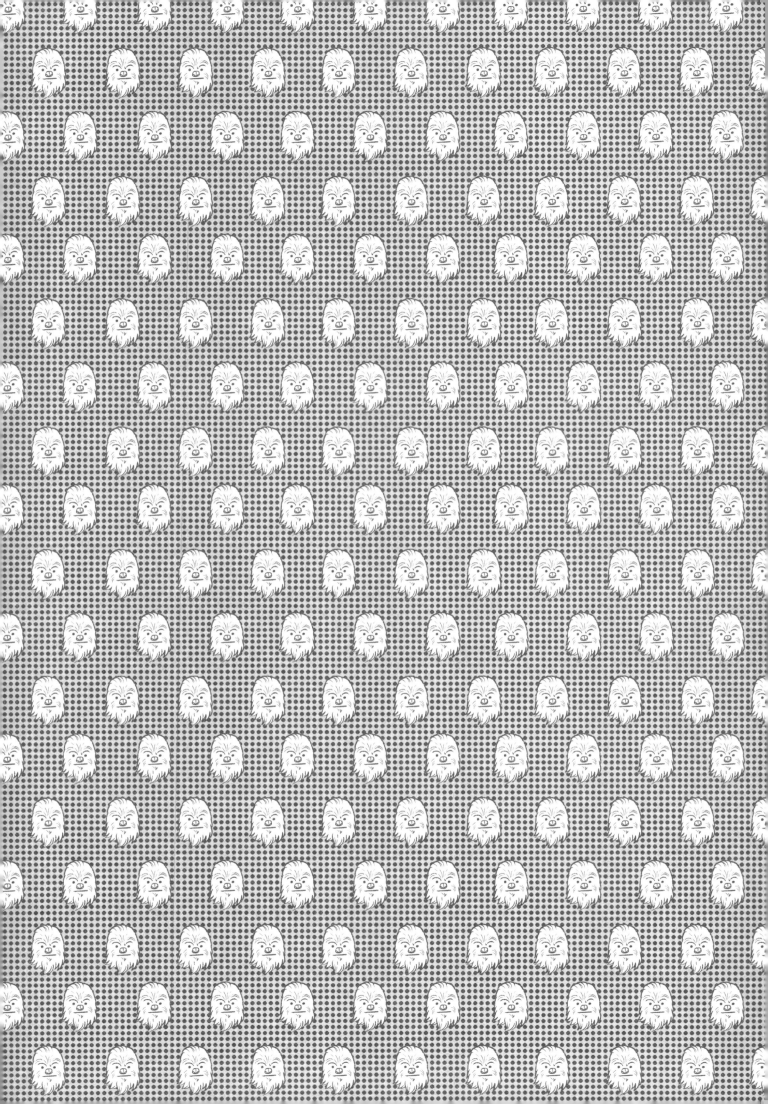

EGMONT

We bring stories to life

First published in Great Britain 2019 by Egmont UK Limited
The Yellow Building, 1 Nicholas Road, London W11 4AN

Illustrations by Ulises Farinas
Colour by Gabriel Cassata
Written by Katrina Pallant
Designed by Richie Hull

© & ™ 2019 Lucasfilm Ltd.
ISBN 978 1 4052 9346 4
70223/001
Printed in Italy

To find more great *Star Wars* books, visit www.egmont.co.uk/starwars

Stay safe online. Any website addresses listed in this book are correct at the time of going to print. However, Egmont is not responsible for content hosted by third parties. Please be aware that online content can be subject to change and websites can contain content that is unsuitable for children. We advise that all children are supervised when using the internet.

Egmont takes its responsibility to the planet and its inhabitants very seriously. We aim to use papers from well-managed forests run by responsible suppliers.

STAR WARS™
WHERE'S THE WOOKIEE? 3

Find this Wookiee!

Search the many locations from the *Star Wars* saga to find this well-known rebel hero. Chewbacca is hiding in every scene along with friends and foes!

CHEWBACCA joined the Rebel Alliance with his lifelong friend Han Solo. The pair flew many important missions in their famous freighter, the *Millennium Falcon*.

Contents

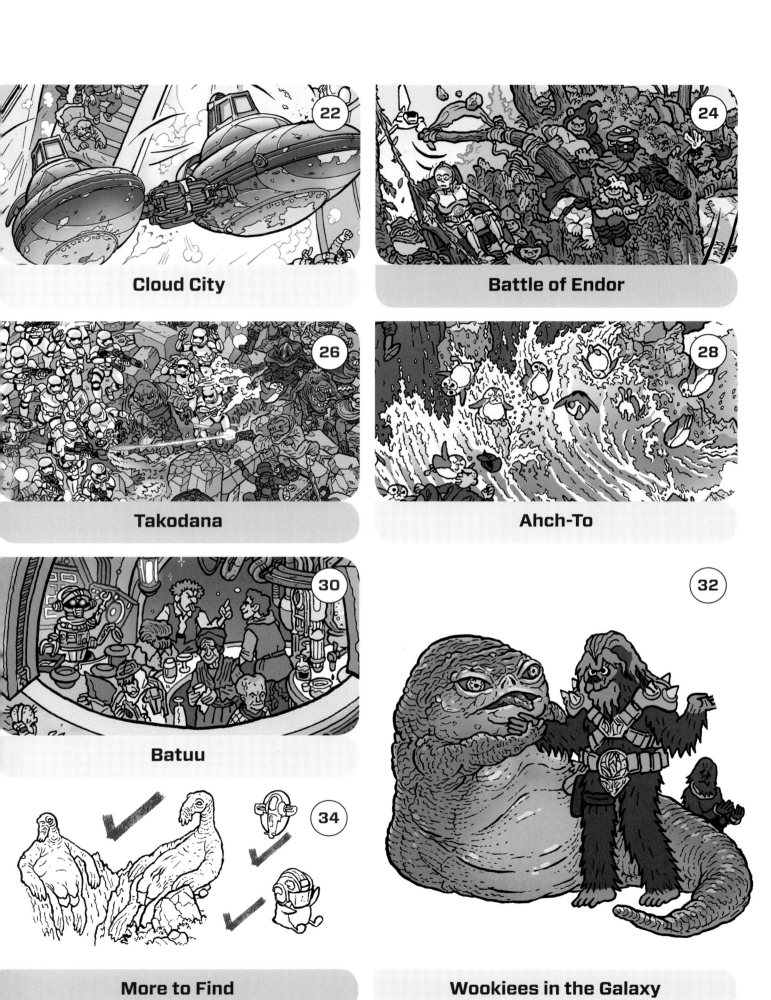

Cloud City 22

Battle of Endor 24

Takodana 26

Ahch-To 28

Batuu 30

32

34

More to Find

Wookiees in the Galaxy

Chewbacca's Journey

Find out about the life of this famous Wookiee.

1. Chewbacca was born on Kashyyyk, the forest-covered home planet of the Wookiees.

2. Chewie commanded forces during the battle of Kashyyyk alongside the Grand Army of the Republic and the great Jedi Master Yoda. Palpatine ordered the clone troopers to take down the Jedi, and Chewie helped Yoda escape.

3. Having been betrayed by a bounty hunter, Chewie ended up in the custody of the Empire on Mimban, where he was kept shackled in a muddy prison. Here he met Han Solo, a rogue Corellian who would become Chewie's lifelong friend. The two escaped and joined Tobias Beckett's gang.

4. Chewie travelled to Vandor with Beckett's gang to steal coaxium for the crime boss Dryden Vos.

5. After the failed heist on Vandor, the group travelled to Kessel. Here many Wookiees had been enslaved to work the spice mines. Chewie worked to free his kin but chose to stay with Han instead of travelling back to Kashyyyk with them.

6. Chewbacca took the seat as co-pilot on the *Falcon* for the first time when Han made the Kessel Run in a legendary 12 parsecs.

7. On Numidian Prime Han won the *Falcon* from Lando Calrissian in a game of sabacc and he and Chewie set off for a life as smugglers.

8. Chewbacca met Obi-Wan in the cantina in Mos Eisley. He and Han offered the Jedi Master passage to Alderaan on the *Falcon* for a large sum of money.

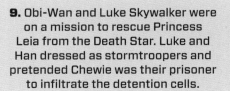

9. Obi-Wan and Luke Skywalker were on a mission to rescue Princess Leia from the Death Star. Luke and Han dressed as stormtroopers and pretended Chewie was their prisoner to infiltrate the detention cells.

10. Luke hoped Han and Chewie would stay and help the rebels destroy the Death Star. Chewie tried to convince his friend to do the right thing, but Han wanted to leave to settle a debt he owed the crime lord Jabba the Hutt. The duo returned just in time to protect Luke from Vader's TIE fighter, allowing the young Jedi to fire proton torpedoes into the Death Star's exhaust point, claiming victory for the Rebellion.

11. As members of the Rebel Alliance, Han and Chewie travelled to the new rebel base on Hoth. While on patrol, Han destroyed an Imperial probe droid but could not stop it from transmitting the base's location back to the Empire. Chewie, Han, Leia and C-3PO were forced to flee in the *Falcon* from the resulting Imperial assault.

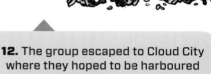

12. The group escaped to Cloud City where they hoped to be harboured by Han's old friend Lando. They grew increasingly suspicious, especially after C-3PO disappeared. Chewie went to find the droid, discovering him in pieces.

13. After Han was captured by Vader, Boba Fett took him to Jabba to settle his debt. Leia used Chewie to infiltrate the Hutt's palace on Tatooine. The group were imprisoned, but Luke arrived to rescue them all.

14. Chewie joined the rebel strike team heading for Endor to take down the second Death Star's shield generator. Chewie took out an Imperial scout with his bowcaster. The group were captured, but were saved when the Ewoks joined the fight.

15. Years later, Chewie and Han returned to their smuggling life. They boarded the *Falcon*, which was stolen from them, to find Rey and Finn hiding in a smuggling compartment. The two were trying to return the droid BB-8 to the Resistance. Han and Chewie agreed to help.

16. Han, Chewie and their new friends travelled to Takodana to see an old friend, Maz Kanata. Unfortunately they were spotted by a First Order spy and had to fight a battle against invading troops.

17. The group were rescued by the Resistance and Chewie was happy to be reunited with his old friend Leia. Han and Chewie agreed to join Finn on a mission to Starkiller Base.

Han and Chewie set the charges to destroy the Starkiller's defences, but were interrupted by the arrival of Han's estranged son, Kylo Ren. Chewie was enraged and heartbroken when Ren killed his father, and the Wookiee shot Ren.

18. Rey duelled with Kylo Ren as the Starkiller exploded around them, and Chewie arrived to help Rey and Finn escape just in time.

19. Chewie went with Rey and R2-D2 to Ahch-To to find Luke Skywalker, who had been in self-imposed exile. While Rey trained with the old Jedi Master, Chewie stayed with the *Falcon* and met some inquisitive little birds named porgs.

20. Chewie co-piloted the *Falcon* with the remaining members of the Resistance after a tense battle on Crait. On Batuu, Hondo made a deal with Chewie to borrow the *Falcon* to use in a smuggling run to Corellia.

Friends and Foes

Here are the characters to search for in the busy *Star Wars* locations...

 B8G-HOR is a labour droid who is part of a slave uprising on Kessel. B8G-HOR is freed from his restraining bolts and joins a mob of other droids to attack their captors.

 GREBE-KORORA is a Lanai, who lives on the remote planet of Ahch-To. The males of his species spend their time hunting and fishing to feed the females back home.

 BLACK KRRSANTAN is a Wookiee bounty hunter who is often employed by Jabba the Hutt. He is highly skilled in combat and is even a match against his fellow Wookiees.

 HAN SOLO is a smuggler and rebel hero. Flying his famous ship the *Millennium Falcon* with co-pilot Chewbacca, Solo has been present at many major rebel victories.

 DARTH VADER is the greatest villain of the Galactic Empire. A former Jedi turned to the dark side, Vader serves the Emperor and aims to destroy the Rebellion.

 HESPER-INGUZA is another male Lanai. The males only return home once a month, and are greeted by a celebration with music and dancing, which lasts for many days.

 DJ R-3X is a former pilot of a Starspeeder 3000 for Star Tours. Today, he can be found playing the latest hits from around the galaxy in the heart of Black Spire Outpost.

 HONDO OHNAKA led a Weequay pirate gang during the Clone Wars. Despite his greed and criminal tendencies, Hondo also aided the Rebellion from time to time.

 **DOK-ONDAR** is an Ithorian collector who operates an antique store on Batuu. He loves a good deal, and only sells his treasure to customers who offer the right price.

 L3-37 is a one-of-a-kind, self-modified droid who flies alongside Lando on the *Falcon*. She is very vocal for droids rights, and helps lead a rebellion of slave droids on Kessel.

 FINN joins the Resistance after escaping his life as a First Order stormtrooper. Now spending his time with new heroic friends, he hopes to leave the past behind him.

 LANDO CALRISSIAN is a smooth-talking smuggler who lost the *Falcon* to Han Solo in a bet. He is drawn in to the rebels' fight and helps destroy the second Death Star.

 FUGAS FANDITA is a terrifying-looking Gotarite, who serves the Mining Guild on Vandor. He is a frequent visitor to the gambling hall in the planet's famous saloon.

 **LARK AND JONK** are a Danzikan who play sabacc on Vandor. Nicknamed 'the Twins', this two-headed creature must participate as one player to avoid cheating.

 GLAUCUS is an Octeroid who can regularly be seen around the sabacc table. He prefers to watch the game because other players can see his cards reflected in his big eye.

 LEIA ORGANA is princess of Alderaan, daughter of Anakin Skywalker and prominent rebel ally. She helps steal the Death Star plans, striking a heavy blow to the Empire.

 GRAND MOFF TARKIN is a ruthless senior officer in the Empire. He is put in charge of Death Star operations after becoming a fast favourite of the Emperor.

 LOBOT is Baron Administrator Lando's aide on Cloud City. Lobot has a brain enhancement that allows him to communicate directly with computers.

LOGRAY is the medicine man of the Bright Tree tribe. He is reluctant to follow the tribe into danger, but he is eventually convinced to join the fight against the Empire.

LOHGARRA is captain of the *Mighty Oak Apocalypse*. She used to transport cargo trying to stay on the right side of the law, but eventually joined the rebel cause.

LUKE SKYWALKER is a great Jedi knight and rebel hero. This farmboy turned X-wing pilot is responsible for the critical shot that destroyed the Empire's Death Star.

MAZ KANATA lives in an ancient castle on Takodana, where she welcomes travelling smugglers to reside. Maz is over 1000 years old and is knowledgeable about the Jedi.

NIEN NUNB is a key ally to the Rebel Alliance. Originally a smuggler, Nien Nunb's excellent piloting skills come in handy during key missions against the Empire.

OBI-WAN KENOBI is a great Jedi Master. He was trained by Qui-Gon Jinn, and took Anakin Skywalker as his Padawan. Kenobi also became a mentor to Luke Skywalker.

PAPLOO is a skilled Ewok scout. He steals a speeder bike belonging to Imperial scout troopers, distracting them and giving the rebels time to get to the shield generator.

QI'RA is a childhood friend of Han Solo, and now the most trusted lieutenant of ruthless crime boss, Dryden Vos. Well trained in martial arts, Qi'ra is a deadly opponent.

REY is a Force-sensitive human from Jakku. She joins the Resistance after the First Order comes to her home planet, and trains with Luke Skywalker in the ways of the Jedi.

RIO DURANT is a member of Beckett's crew. This four-armed Ardennian is an excellent pilot and tactician, regularly helping the gang out of tight spots.

SAGWA is one of many Wookiees imprisoned on Kessel to work the mines. Chewie arrives as part of a heist and helps Sagwa start a revolt against the slavers.

SENNA is a Gigoran who was enslaved on Kessel by the Pyke Syndicate. He was captured for his superior strength, but eventually breaks out during a slave revolt.

SIDON ITHANO, also known as the Crimson Corsair, is a pirate who wears a distinctive Kaleesh helmet. He and his first mate Quiggold frequently visit Maz's Castle.

TARFFUL is a brave and loyal Wookiee Chieftan. He serves as a general during the Clone Wars, fighting alongside Chewie at the battle of Kashyyyk.

THROMBA is a Frigosian cryptosurgeon, who works with her partner Laparo out of Maz Kanata's castle. The duo perform cosmetic surgery on criminal clients.

TOBIAS BECKETT leads a crew of professional thieves, who perform heists and scams. Beckett meets Solo and Chewie on Mimban and brings them along on a job.

ULIBACCA is a long time friend of Chewbacca. He runs an art school on Kashyyyk and his work is in many art galleries throughout the galaxy.

VAL is the most capable member of Beckett's crew. She is a crackshot with a blaster rifle and extremely brave, ultimately sacrificing herself for the group.

WICKET, an Ewok, is a member of the Bright Tree tribe on Endor. He helps Leia and the other rebels to destroy the second Death Star's protective shield.

YODA is a legendary Jedi Grand Master, whose wisdom and experience guided many young Jedi in the ways of the Force. Despite his small size, Yoda is an expert in combat.

KASHYYYK

Home of the great Wookiee race, this forest planet is full of life. The Wookiees are having a celebration for Life Day – a holiday to honour Wookiee culture and harmony – and all the tribes are in attendance.

Black Krrsantan

Lohgarra

Tarfful

Ulibacca

Mimban

This muddy planet has been a site of conflict for many years due to its mineral resources. Here, a young Han Solo is framed as an Imperial deserter and thrown in a pit, where he meets his hairy lifelong friend for the first time.

Corporal Han Solo

Beckett

Rio

Val

Vandor Lodge

This lodge draws travellers from all over looking for a game of cards, to catch a droid fight or to listen to the resident band. The bustling saloon on the cold planet of Vandor plays host to notorious card cheat, Lando Calrissian.

Fugas Fandita

Glaucus

Qi'ra

Lark and Jonk

Kessel

Rich in spice and coaxium, most of the planet is given over to large mining operations. These are kept going by the employment of slave labourers, including a large number of the famously-strong Wookiee race.

Senna　　Sagwa　　B8G-HOR　　L3-37

Death Star

The Empire's greatest superweapon is fully operational, but there are a few unwanted guests on board. A former Jedi Master is here to help the rebel cause yet must avoid some old enemies in the process.

Princess Leia

Darth Vader

Grand Moff Tarkin

Obi-Wan Kenobi

Cloud City

The city in the sky is bustling with activity and industry. This Bespin hub welcomes citizens from all over the galaxy, including an unfortunate rebel droid. C-3PO has met his match, ending up in six pieces, which have been hidden all over Cloud City.

Lando

Lobot

Darth Vader

C-3PO

Battle of Endor

The war between the Rebellion and the Empire has disrupted this quiet Endor forest. The Ewoks of Bright Tree Village have joined the rebels to defeat the invading stormtroopers. These furry friends need to get creative to take down the Imperial walkers!

Wicket

Luke Skywalker

Paploo

Logray

Takodana

Imperials invade the peaceful surrounds of Maz's Castle in the hopes of catching key Resistance allies. Maz's patrons love a good battle and have jumped into the fray.

Finn   Maz Kanata   Thromba   Sidon Ithano

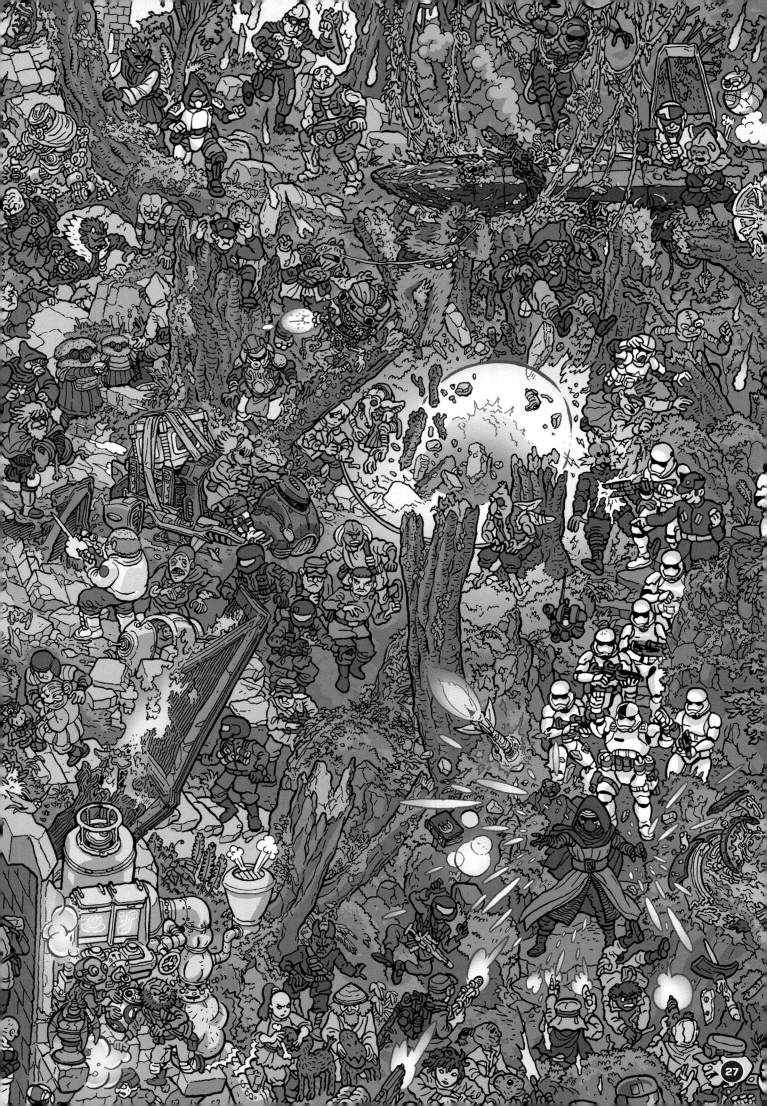

Ahch-To

On a remote planet in the Unknown Regions, a group of curious native birds cause mischief and mayhem. The porgs have the run of the rocky islands, shared by the caretakers who look after the historic structures.

Grebe-Korora   Hesper-Inguza   Yoda   Rey

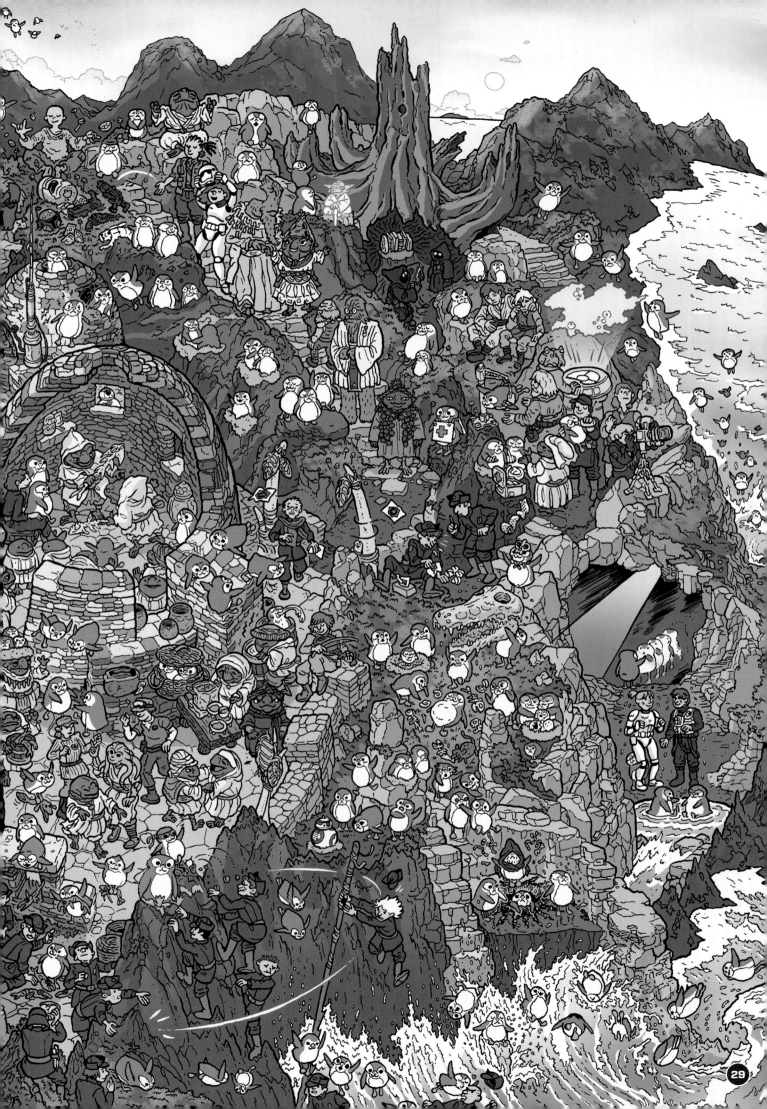

Batuu

A remote outpost on the galaxy's edge, Batuu is notable for the lush trees and mountain spires that decorate its surface. Once a busy crossroads, Batuu is now a thriving port for smugglers and adventurers. Significantly, it has also become a safe haven for those looking to avoid the attention of the First Order.

Hondo Ohnaka

Dok-Ondar

Nien Nunb

DJ R-3X

Wookiees in the Galaxy

Here are some other famous members of the mighty Wookiee race.

Lohgarra

Lohgarra operated a legal cargo business for over 200 years, avoiding the wrath of the Empire that her fellow Wookiees faced. She hired an Imperial defector to join her crew, and when he left to join the Rebellion Lohgarra was reminded of the plight of her people. Eventually, she and her crew joined the Alliance Fleet, and flew the *Mighty Oak Apocalypse* into the Battle of Endor.

Black Krrsantan

This bounty hunter was regularly employed by Jabba the Hutt. He was an exceptional fighter and a dangerous adversary to his opponents. After the Battle of Yavin, Black Krrsantan was hired by Darth Vader to hunt down an agent of the Emperor.

Hailing from the forest-covered planet of Kashyyyk, Wookiees build their homes in the planet's trees.

Gungi

Gungi was training to be a Jedi during the Clone Wars. He was one of the top of his class and was instructed by Yoda to find his kyber crystal in order to construct his lightsaber.

Sagwa

Sagwa was a heroic Wookiee who selflessly helped his fellow enslaved workers by taking on the most difficult tasks. When Han Solo and Chewbacca arrived on Kessel for a smuggling mission, they helped start an uprising among the Wookiees who had been enslaved by the Galactic Empire. Sagwa helped Chewie so that everyone could escape.

Each Wookiee builds their own unique bowcaster, the traditional weapon of this species.

Wullffwarro

Wullffwarro was taken as a slave by the Galactic Empire. He and his son Kitwarr were forced to work the spice mines of Kessel, before being rescued by the crew of the *Ghost*.

Tarfful

This giant Wookiee, aided by the Grand Army of the Republic, led the Wookiees against invading Separatist droid forces. When the Emperor activated Order 66, which saw the Republic clone troopers turn on the Jedi, Tarfful helped Yoda escape from Kashyyyk.

Wookiees are extremely honourable with a code that says they can not use their sharp claws in combat.

More to Find

Now that you've found Chewie, go back to find some of these other items.

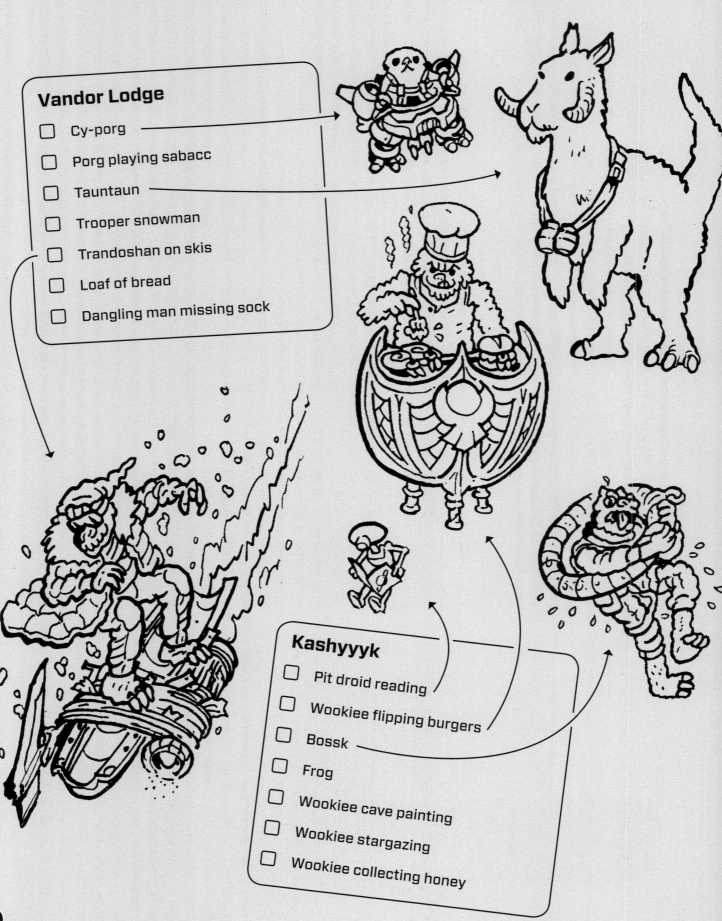

Vandor Lodge

- ☐ Cy-porg
- ☐ Porg playing sabacc
- ☐ Tauntaun
- ☐ Trooper snowman
- ☐ Trandoshan on skis
- ☐ Loaf of bread
- ☐ Dangling man missing sock

Kashyyyk

- ☐ Pit droid reading
- ☐ Wookiee flipping burgers
- ☐ Bossk
- ☐ Frog
- ☐ Wookiee cave painting
- ☐ Wookiee stargazing
- ☐ Wookiee collecting honey

Batuu

- [ ] Baby Trandoshan enjoying a bedtime story
- [ ] Baby Hutt
- [ ] Gonk droid
- [ ] Two aliens sharing a sandwich
- [ ] Gungan licking a menu
- [ ] Stormtrooper reading *Where's the Wookiee?*
- [ ] Family of Bith on holiday

Mimban

- [ ] Sullustan officer
- [ ] Stormtrooper doodle
- [ ] Air traffic controller
- [ ] Trooper with binoculars
- [ ] Gliding Mimbanese
- [ ] Mud trooper with a spade
- [ ] Entrance to escape tunnel

Kessel

- [ ] Trooper parachuting in
- [ ] Quay Tolsite
- [ ] Man drinking from pipe water
- [ ] *Falcon* hologram
- [ ] Sullustan mechanics
- [ ] R5 unit
- [ ] Bith with an eye patch

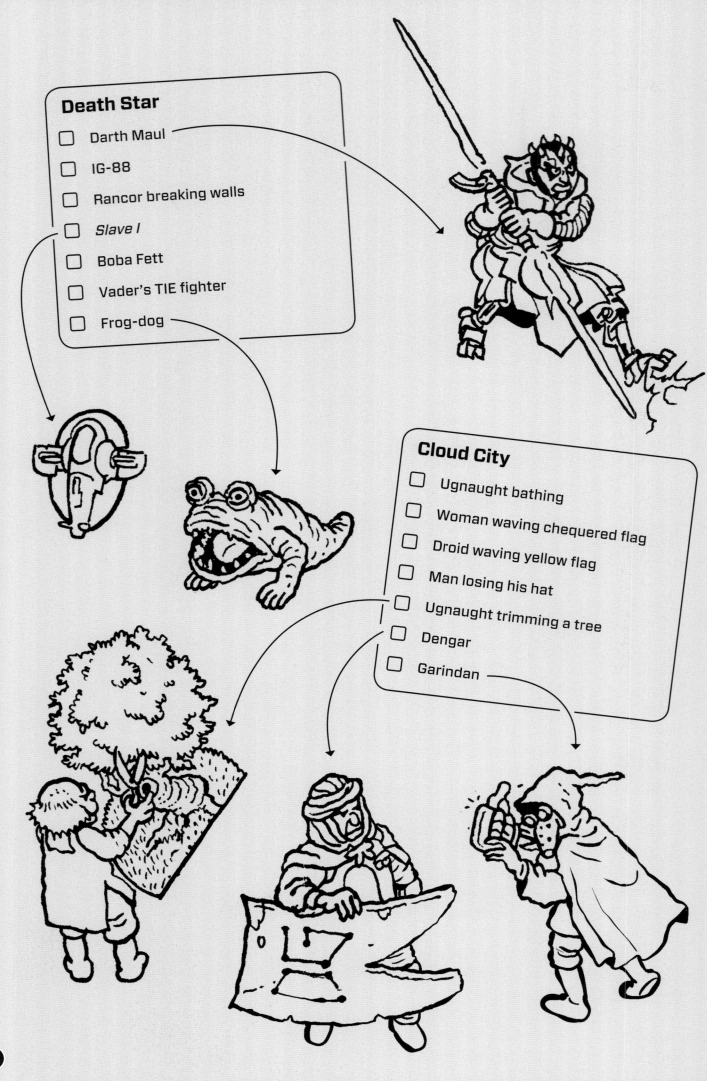

Death Star

- [ ] Darth Maul
- [ ] IG-88
- [ ] Rancor breaking walls
- [ ] *Slave I*
- [ ] Boba Fett
- [ ] Vader's TIE fighter
- [ ] Frog-dog

Cloud City

- [ ] Ugnaught bathing
- [ ] Woman waving chequered flag
- [ ] Droid waving yellow flag
- [ ] Man losing his hat
- [ ] Ugnaught trimming a tree
- [ ] Dengar
- [ ] Garindan

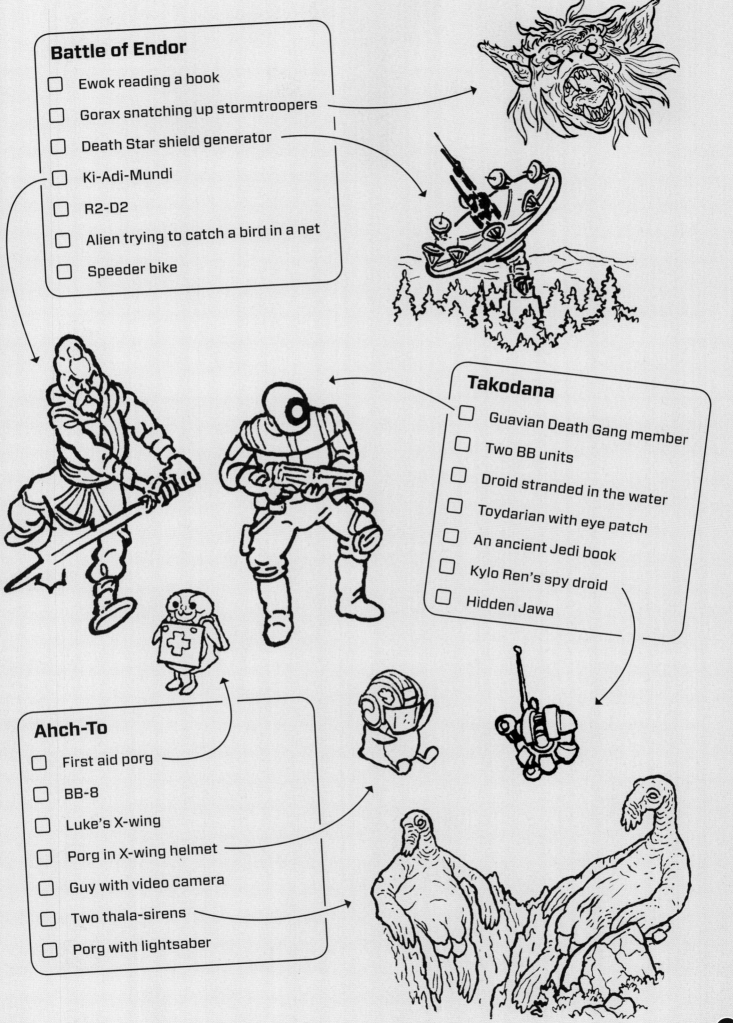

Battle of Endor

- [ ] Ewok reading a book
- [ ] Gorax snatching up stormtroopers
- [ ] Death Star shield generator
- [ ] Ki-Adi-Mundi
- [ ] R2-D2
- [ ] Alien trying to catch a bird in a net
- [ ] Speeder bike

Takodana

- [ ] Guavian Death Gang member
- [ ] Two BB units
- [ ] Droid stranded in the water
- [ ] Toydarian with eye patch
- [ ] An ancient Jedi book
- [ ] Kylo Ren's spy droid
- [ ] Hidden Jawa

Ahch-To

- [ ] First aid porg
- [ ] BB-8
- [ ] Luke's X-wing
- [ ] Porg in X-wing helmet
- [ ] Guy with video camera
- [ ] Two thala-sirens
- [ ] Porg with lightsaber

Answers

Kashyyyk

Mimban

Vandor Lodge

Kessel

Death Star

Battle of
Endor

Takodana

Ahch-To

atuu

TICK OFF THE
CHARACTERS YOU
HAVE FOUND ALONG
THE WAY!